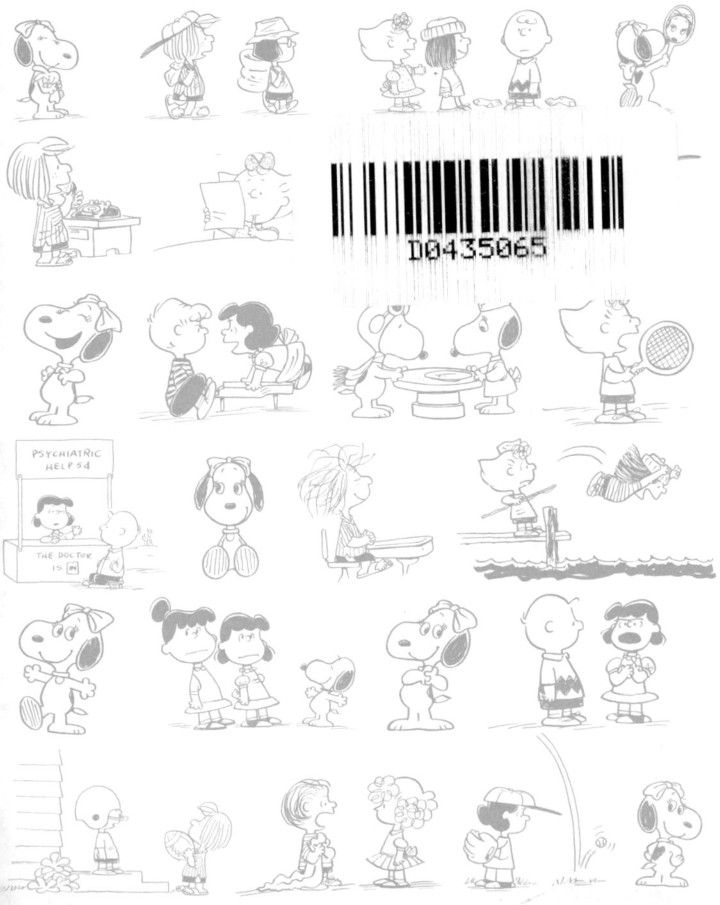
PSYCHIATRIC HELP 5¢
THE DOCTOR IS IN

Be AWESOME

PEANUTS WISDOM TO CARRY YOU THROUGH

Running Press Kids
Hachette Book Group
1290 Avenue of the Americas, New York, NY 10104
www.runningpress.com/rpkids
@RP_Kids

Printed in China

First Edition: March 2015

Published by Running Press Kids, an imprint of Perseus Books, LLC, a subsidiary of Hachette Book Group, Inc. The Running Press Kids name and logo is a trademark of the Hachette Book Group.

The Hachette Speakers Bureau provides a wide range of authors for speaking events. To find out more, go to www.hachettespeakersbureau.com or call (866) 376-6591.

The publisher is not responsible for websites (or their content) that are not owned by the publisher.

Artwork created by Charles M. Schulz
For Charles M. Schulz Creative Associates: pencils by Vicki Scott, inks by Paige Braddock, colors by Donna Almendrala
Print book cover and interior design by T.L. Bonaddio

Library of Congress Control Number: 2014943442

ISBN: 978-0-7624-5593-5 (hardcover)

1010

13   12   11   10   9   8   7   6   5   4

PEANUTS

Be AWESOME

PEANUTS WISDOM TO CARRY YOU THROUGH

Based on the comic strip, PEANUTS,
by Charles M. Schulz

RUNNING PRESS
PHILADELPHIA

"They say that we girls are like beautiful music ... we are like songs one cannot forget."

—*Lucy*

Be
SHARP

Lucy: Are we supposed to yell "I got it!" or "I have it!"?

Charlie Brown: It doesn't matter, Lucy.

Lucy: I think he's right. If you don't got it, you don't have it!

Be
Speculative

"We have to write a book report on Peter Rabbit for school. I may even bring in some speculations on his home life which could prove to be quite interesting. All in all I hope to uncover some truths about our culture."

—*Sally*

Be

DARING

Be
HONEST

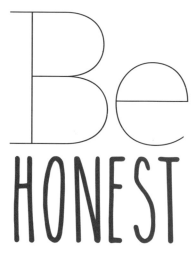

Snoopy: Hey, what happened to all the doughnuts?

Belle: You ate them!

Be
INSPIRING

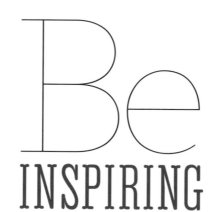

Lucy: Most great composers were inspired by women. Do I inspire you, Schroeder?

Schroeder: You'd inspire me a lot if you'd just go away!

Lucy: I'm afraid you're doomed to be a failure.

Be

Thoughtful

"Yes, Ma'am, I picked them myself. Do we have a vase around here? That's alright, Ma'am, I'll find a place to put them."

—*Marcie*

Be
MARVELOUS

Be
FANTASTIQUE

Be
CHOOSY

Violet: All the boys around here are so dumb! I'd like to meet someone I could really admire.

Lucy: I'd like to meet someone who is honest, has a good sense of humor, is cute, and is sensitive.

Snoopy: Joe Perfect!

Be
KIND

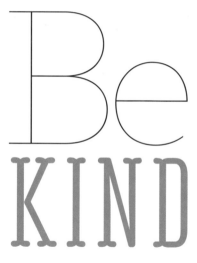

Frieda: Do you always drag that blanket around behind you, Linus?

Linus: As a matter of fact, I do! I suppose you're gonna start in on me now?

Frieda: No, I think it's a good idea . . . I mean, if it makes you feel more secure. Then you should carry it with you.

Be

Carefree

Be

DETERMINED

"It's my life, and I'll do whatever I want with it! I'm my own person!"

—*Lucy*

Be Charming

Eudora: I'm delighted to meet you, Charles. And I hope that we become very good friends.

Sally: See? Just like I told you, she can charm your socks off!

Be SMART

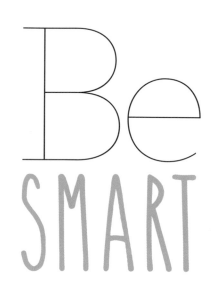

"I guess I learned something, Marcie . . . never give your heart to a blockhead."

—*Peppermint Patty*

Be
PROUD

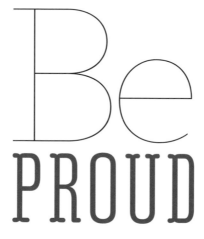

"I'm proud of being crabby ... The crabby little girls of today are the crabby old women of tomorrow!"

—*Lucy*

Be
FEISTY

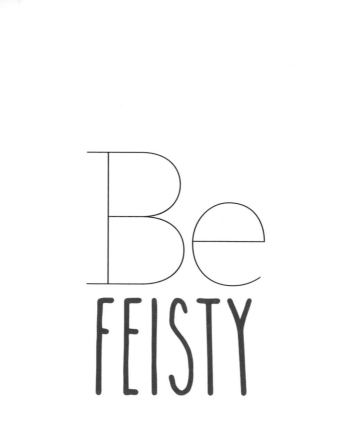

Be SPORTY

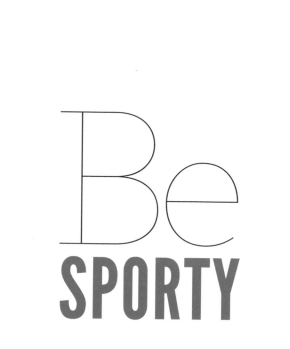

Sally: Okay, I'm ready . . . but hit it to my forehand. Don't hit it to my funny side.

Charlie Brown: Backhand.

Sally: Whatever!

Be

Exceptional

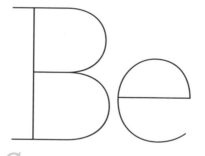

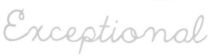

"Well, I'll never be beautiful, ma'am. Therefore, I'm trying a new approach. I'm into 'cute'!"

—*Peppermint Patty*

Be
FORWARD-THINKING

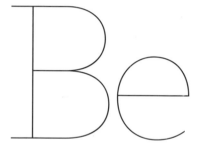

Be
BLUNT

Peppermint Patty: I need your help, Chuck. Our team has a ballgame today, but one of our players is going to be missing and. . . .

Charlie Brown: You mean you want me to play for your team?

Peppermint Patty: No, we just want to know if we can borrow your glove.

Be
APPRECIATIVE

"We need to study the lives of great women like my grandmother. Talk to your own grandmother today. Ask her questions. You'll find she knows more than peanut butter cookies!"

　　—*Lucy*

Be

Helpful

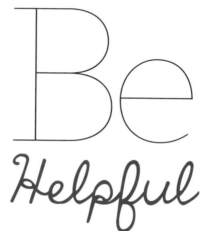

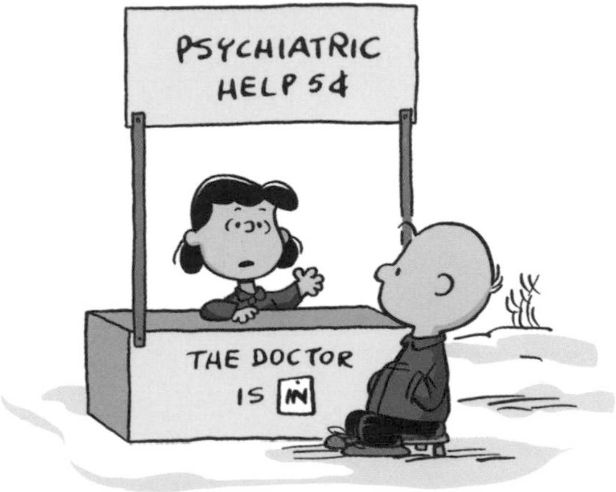
PSYCHIATRIC
HELP 5¢
THE DOCTOR
IS IN

Charlie Brown: Nothing ever goes right for me.

Lucy: I've been thinking about that a lot, Charlie Brown. Maybe you're your own worst enemy.

Be
ACCURATE

"It's a scientific fact that at our age girls are
smarter than boys!"

—*Violet*

Be
ENERGETIC

Be
COMPLEX

"I know from personal experience that it would take a genius to understand me!"

—*Lucy*

Be
Mysterious

Be Presentable

Be ADVENTUROUS

Peppermint Patty: I hope that tent doesn't get too heavy for you, Marcie.

Marcie: This isn't a tent, Sir . . . these are marshmallows.

Be
CONFIDENT

Charlie Brown: Do you know exactly what you're going to be when you grow up?

Lucy: Of course. A smart cookie!

Be
DYNAMIC

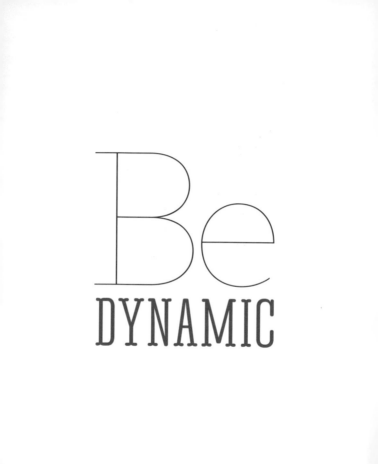

"My dad bought me this helmet, sir. He says girls can play sports just as well as boys can."

—Marcie

Be

Curious

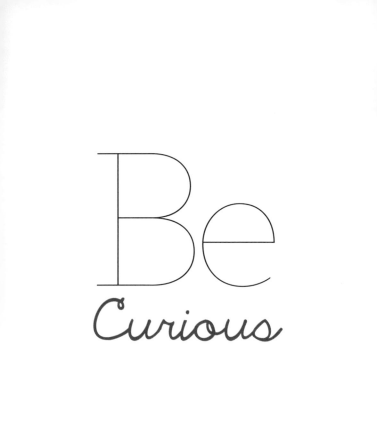

"This is my report on Autumn. Some people call it Fall. If leaves fall in Autumn, do leaves Autumn in Fall?"

—*Sally*

Be FUNNY

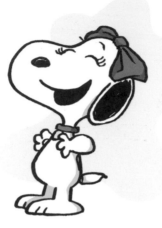

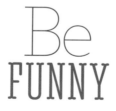

Be
WARM

Be
CHARGED

Be

Loving

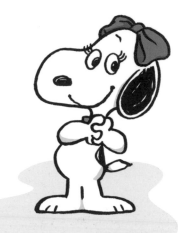

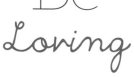

Be
Happy

Be

VISIONARY

"I have a vision, Chuck. I can see the day coming when women will have the same opportunities in sports as men!"

—*Peppermint Patty*

Be
YOURSELF!

Marcie: Life has its sunshine and rain, Sir . . . its days and its nights . . . its peaks and its valleys. . . .

Peppermint Patty: It's raining tonight in my valley!

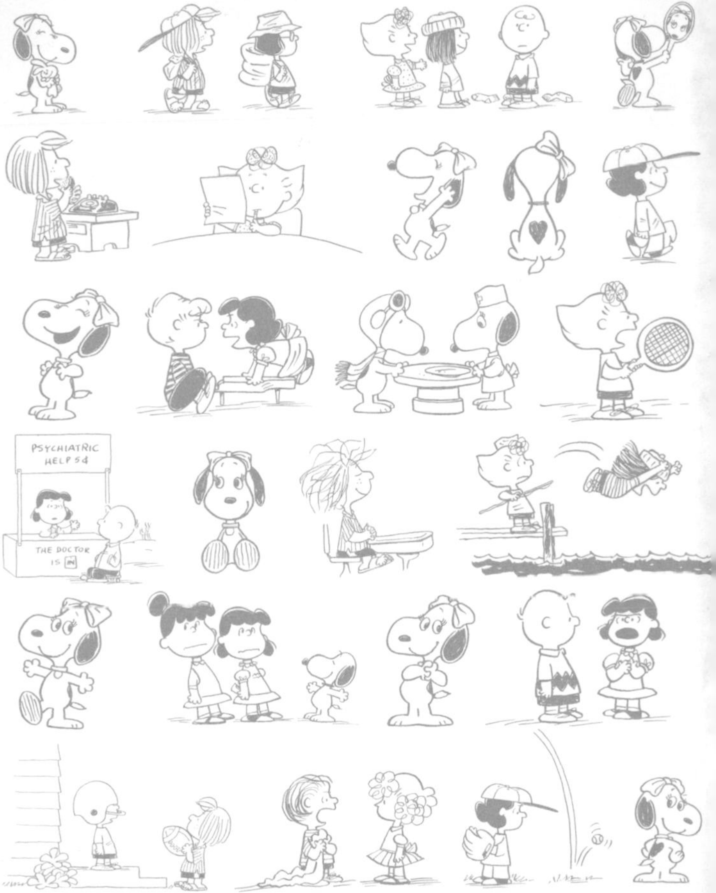
PSYCHIATRIC HELP 5¢
THE DOCTOR IS IN